An Adams' Wood Mystery

WHO BROKE THE MIRROR?

Follow the clues and find the answer

To: Christopher Micheal Ian

From: Daddy

Written by Stewart Cowley
Illustrated by Susi Adams

DERRYDALE BOOKS
NEW YORK

Published 1986 by Derrydale Books,
distributed by Crown Publishers, Inc.

Produced for Derrydale Books by
Victoria House Publishing Ltd.
4/5 Lower Borough Walls
Bath BA1 1QR, England

Printed in Belgium

Welcome to Adams' Wood

"Hello, I'm Holmes Mouse, the great detective!"

"And I'm Watson Mouse, his best friend!"

This is a story about the day of the Fair at Adams' Wood. Everybody had a lovely time—until one of the funny mirrors got broken. Can you help us find out who did it?

Read the story and look at the pictures carefully to find the clues. We will be looking for clues, too—watch out for us.

If you don't solve the mystery, we've put together all the evidence in one big picture near the end of the book . . . and if you still don't know who broke the mirror, we may have found the answer for you.

The day of the Fair had finally come to Adams' Wood, and everyone was looking forward to it. Floppy was one of the first to get there and he raced through the wood with a big balloon.

"Look at me," called Bobtail, from the swings, "I'm flying!" He did look funny. As he went higher and higher his ears blew back in the wind!

"The swings are too high for me," said Mr. Raccoon.
He liked the merry-go-round best, and soon he was
swooping and spinning in a wonderful, painted airplane.

Mrs. Duck liked the merry-go-round too. Her favorite was the bright red train. "I'll just have one more turn!" she called, as she whizzed by for the fourth time.

The young mice were having lots of fun on the slide.
"Look out!" they shouted, as they took turns zooming
down. "We'll go even faster next time," they laughed,
climbing to the top again.

Whoosh! Down the slide went
Longtail—right into Robbie Raccoon.
"Sorry Robbie," panted Longtail. "I
couldn't stop!"

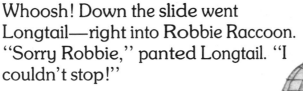

"Look out, Longtail,
you almost knocked
Robbie over!"

Harry Hedgehog was excited. He'd won a prize—a
shiny, new spinning-top. "It's lovely," said Billy Beaver.
"Let's make it spin!"

Sammy Squirrel was winning prizes,
too. He'd already won a coconut and
was trying hard for another.

"You're doing well,
Sammy, but watch where
you're throwing that ball!"

Mrs. Fox was taking a turn at the ring-toss booth.
"Almost!" she cried, as a ring spun across the table.
"Maybe I'll win a cake!" There were always lots of good
things to eat at the fair.

Mr. Squirrel had bought some candy
apples, which he was now handing out.
"This one's for Sammy," he said. "But,
where is he?"

"It's not like Sammy
to miss a treat!"

At one edge of the wood there was a Hall of Mirrors.
One mirror made you look fat, another made you look
thin. "Look at me in this funny mirror!" laughed
Mrs. Hedgehog. "Let's try another."

"Here are some more mirrors!" called Mr. Beaver.
Suddenly he gave a shout. "Oh no! This one's broken!
Who could have done it?"

"Who could that ball belong to?"

Mrs. Mouse and Mr. Frog ran over to see what was happening. "Look!" cried Mr. Frog. He bent down and picked something out of the grass. It was a ball!

"I've found a coconut!" called Mrs.
Beaver. "But what is it doing here?"
"I think I can guess," shouted Mr. Frog.
"Come on, everyone!"

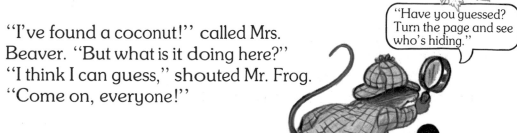

"Have you guessed?
Turn the page and see
who's hiding."